# The Emperor's New Clothes

## A Story About Honesty

D1209383

Library of Congress Cataloging-in-Publication Data
Names: Rusu, Meredith, adapter. | Arbat, Carles, 1973- illustrator. |
    Andersen, H. C. (Hans Christian), 1805-1875. Keiserens nye klæder.
    English.
Title: The emperor's new clothes : a story about honesty / adapted by
    Meredith Rusu ; illustrated by Carles Arbat.
Description: New York : Children's Press, an imprint of Scholastic, 2020. |
    Series: Tales to grow by | Summary: A retelling of the classic story
    emphasizing the role of honesty in exposing the fraud of the two thieves
    and their invisible clothes. With questions and guidelines for parents
    and educators.
Identifiers: LCCN 2019034151 | ISBN 9780531231906 (library binding) | ISBN
    9780531246245 (paperback)
Subjects: LCSH: Andersen, H. C. (Hans Christian), 1805-1875. Keiserens nye
    klæder--Adaptations. | Honesty--Juvenile fiction. | Clothing and
    dress--Juvenile fiction. | Fairy tales. | CYAC: Fairy tales. |
    Honesty--Fiction. | Clothing and dress--Fiction. | LCGFT: Fairy tales.
Classification: LCC PZ8.R8983 Em 2020 | DDC [E]--dc23

Design by Book & Look

# The Emperor's New Clothes

## A Story About Honesty

Adapted by
**Meredith Rusu**

Illustrated by
**Carles Arbat**

Expert advice by
**Eva Martínez**

**Children's Press®**
An Imprint of Scholastic Inc.

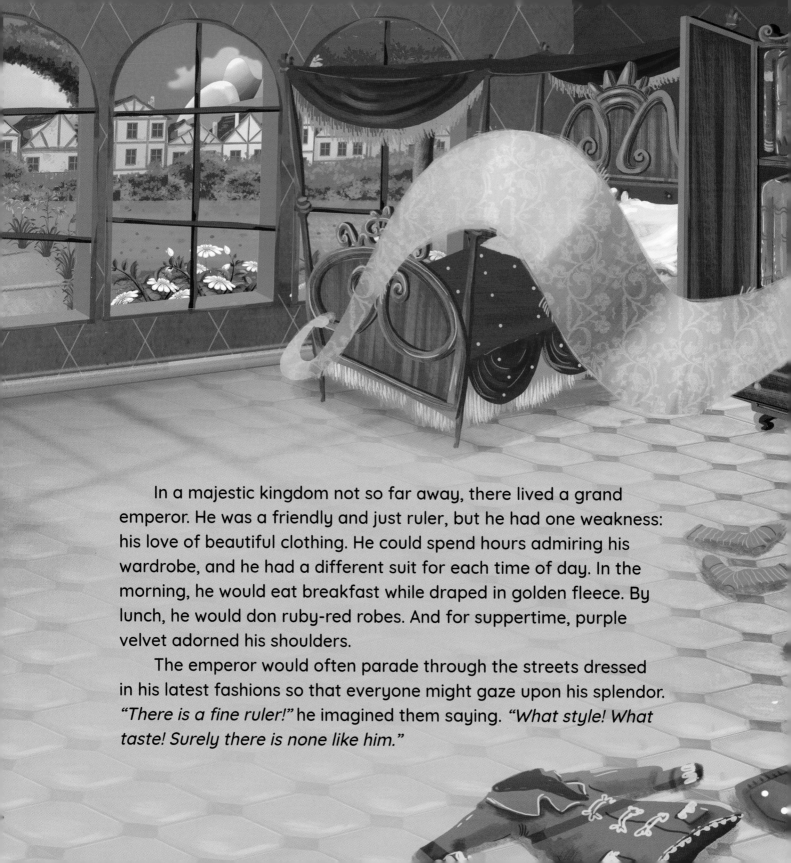

In a majestic kingdom not so far away, there lived a grand emperor. He was a friendly and just ruler, but he had one weakness: his love of beautiful clothing. He could spend hours admiring his wardrobe, and he had a different suit for each time of day. In the morning, he would eat breakfast while draped in golden fleece. By lunch, he would don ruby-red robes. And for suppertime, purple velvet adorned his shoulders.

The emperor would often parade through the streets dressed in his latest fashions so that everyone might gaze upon his splendor. *"There is a fine ruler!"* he imagined them saying. *"What style! What taste! Surely there is none like him."*

One day, two thieves were traveling past the kingdom after having escaped with stolen money and goods from a distant village. They caught sight of the emperor's morning parade, and instantly, a plot began to swirl in their heads.

Now the emperor was fully intrigued. *With an outfit made from such wonderful stuff, everyone would admire my great style anew,* he thought. *And I could tell who in my council is wise or who is unworthy. It would be foolish to pass up such an opportunity.*

So he immediately ordered the thieves to weave as much of the cloth as they could, sparing no expense.

The thieves spent day and night working furiously at their looms. But in reality, they were doing nothing at all. For their hands were empty and their looms bare. They requested fine silk and rich gold thread by the spool, only to pocket them away in their knapsacks and continue weaving thin air.

Have you ever told a little lie to someone who trusted you? How did it make you feel? Do you think the thieves may be a little nervous about not telling the truth?

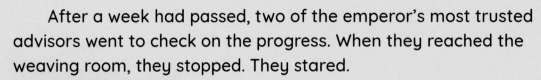

After a week had passed, two of the emperor's most trusted advisors went to check on the progress. When they reached the weaving room, they stopped. They stared.

The looms were empty!

"What do you good gentlemen think?" the thieves asked eagerly. "Is this not the most glorious fabric you have ever seen?"

"I–I don't—" the first advisor stammered. He truly could not see anything there. But he remembered that the cloth would be invisible to those who were unfit for their job. And he certainly didn't want his fellow advisor reporting that back to the emperor.

"I…think it is marvelous!" he said at last.

Now the second advisor trembled. Was he the only one in the room who could not see the fabric? "Oh yes, it is splendid!" he quickly agreed.

Why did the advisors lie and say they could see the fabric when they couldn't?

When the advisors returned and told the emperor how wonderful the cloth was, the emperor could wait no longer. He hurried to see the magnificent fabric himself.

Imagine his surprise when he found he could not see the material at all!

"I don't understand…," the emperor said slowly.

"Is Your Highness not pleased?" the thieves asked, pretending to be very worried. "We have been working day and night. Oh please, tell us you admire the rich colors and patterns. Surely a man of your wisdom must appreciate its splendor!"

Have you ever wanted to believe something even if it seemed too good to be true?

Now the emperor grew extremely concerned. *Could it be that I am not fit to be emperor?* he wondered. *I would never have thought it so. But if I admit I cannot see the very fabric I asked for, the whole kingdom will lose confidence in me.*

So instead, he squared his shoulders. "This is the most superb cloth I have ever seen in my life. You must make me a suit to parade across the kingdom at once. I will pay any price."

Delighted, the thieves agreed. And three days later, they fitted the emperor with a custom-tailored suit made out of nothing at all.

The day of the grand parade arrived. Citizens from all corners of the kingdom lined the streets, eager to catch a glimpse of the cloth that could tell them if they were worthy and wise.

But as the emperor paraded past, the citizens' excited chatter hushed. Uncertain murmurs rippled through the crowd. And people glanced at their neighbors, waiting to see if anyone would confess what was true for all of them—*no one* could see the emperor's new clothes.

What would you have done if you were one of those citizens who could not see the new clothes?

But no one did.

Instead, shouts of praise rang out.

"How wonderful our emperor looks in his new clothes!"

"How fine!" "How splendid!"

For not a single citizen was willing to admit that they were not worthy to see the cloth.

The emperor continued along, all the while followed by cheers and compliments. Off to the side, two parents stood with their young son. He was a small child, and his father raised him upon his shoulders so that he might get a better view. But when the boy saw the emperor, his eyes grew wide.

What do you think the boy felt when everyone else was saying they could see the new clothes that weren't really there? Do you think he had doubts about what he saw?

And then, he blurted out: "Why, he's not wearing anything at all! He's only wearing his underwear!"

The surrounding people gasped.

"Who said that?" one asked. "Who said they cannot see the cloth?"

"It's only a child!" exclaimed another.

"An honest child!" his father insisted. "Perhaps more honest than any of us. A child cannot be unfit for his job. So he must be telling the truth."

Are children more honest than adults? Why?

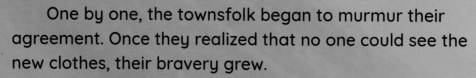

One by one, the townsfolk began to murmur their agreement. Once they realized that no one could see the new clothes, their bravery grew.

"The emperor wears nothing at all!" they cried.

And the emperor himself flushed bright red. Because he realized they were right.

The emperor ordered his advisors to have the thieves immediately banished from the kingdom. All of the fine silk and spun gold they had stolen was retrieved. And the grateful emperor summoned the little boy and his parents before him.

"I owe you a debt of gratitude," the emperor told the young boy. "Your honesty has saved me from making an even bigger fool out of myself than I already have. I thank you."

The little boy shrugged. "My parents told me to always tell the truth," he said.

The emperor smiled. "Then they must be very wise indeed."

Is telling the truth always the best thing to do? Why?

### What does it mean to be honest?

Being honest means telling the truth and not cheating. Honest people show respect for other people's feelings as well as their own.

### What if, sometimes, I tell a little lie?

Have you ever done something sneaky and then later said you didn't? That was a time you told a little lie, called a *fib*. There will be times you may want to fib in order to avoid getting in trouble. But it is always better to tell the truth. In fact, fibbing usually makes things worse. If you're honest from the start, you'll likely get in less trouble. And you'll always feel much better than if you told a lie!

### Should I tell the truth even if it might hurt someone's feelings?

It's important to respect other people's feelings when you're saying what you think or feel. For example, you may think your friend's new haircut is weird-looking, but it's not very kind to tell them so. If you're ever unsure how to tell the truth about something you feel is important, ask a grown-up you trust to help you find the right words.

**Put your honesty to work!**

• If you have done something wrong, admit it. Telling the truth when you make a mistake is the best way to show you are honest.

• If you are playing a game with friends, don't cheat! Everyone deserves the same chance to win.

• If all your friends say they like something, such as a new movie or activity, but you don't feel the same way, don't feel pressured to agree with them just to fit in. Be honest and express your own opinion. You will be fine as long as you do it with respect.

• Don't be afraid to say how you are thinking or feeling. It's okay to admit, "I'm angry," "I'm upset," or "I'm jealous." Just remember to use words that are kind, not hurtful.

**When you tell the truth, your parents, friends, and teachers know they can trust you. It is worth being honest!**

## GUIDELINES FOR FAMILIES AND EDUCATORS

**It takes courage to be honest. When children feel safe in expressing the truth, they learn the power of being trustworthy. As adults, we can help teach the importance of honesty in the way we respond to their behavior—good or bad—and by modeling honesty in our everyday lives.**

Here are some tips to encourage honesty:

• Be patient when your child isn't truthful. It can be hard not to immediately think, *Oh no! My child told a lie! He's a liar!* But telling a lie is a behavior, not a personality trait. It's no different than a temper tantrum. And as with a tantrum, children need encouragement and support to make a better choice the next time.

• Focus on the value of honesty rather than the punishment for lying. Of course, consequences are necessary for dishonest behavior. But once a child does tell the truth, even if it required prompting, praise the courage that the admission took.

• Always affirm your child's feelings. Being honest means understanding one's emotions and knowing how to express them properly.

• When your child is honest about something in an awkward situation, such as saying they don't like the way another person looks, acknowledge their observation while emphasizing the need to respect other people's feelings. Ask your child how they felt and how they think the other person felt. Guide them toward an appropriate expression of their honest perception.

• Until children are six or seven years old, fantasy plays a very important role in their development. Being imaginative is different than telling lies. Listen to their words and try to understand what they need, whether what they're saying is true or not.

• Like all values, honesty is taught by example. Be honest with your little one. You are the role model they will follow.

**Helping children to be honest will make it easier for them to maintain relationships of trust and respect with themselves and with others. The aim should not be avoiding reprimands or punishments, but progressively incorporating honesty and its rewards into their lives.**

Eva Martínez is a teacher and family counselor. She is the author of two books about emotional education for children, and she is a regular contributor to educational magazines in her native Spain.

Enjoy the magic of fairy tales, and continue growing with more books in this series!

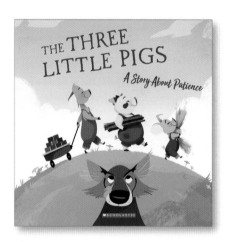

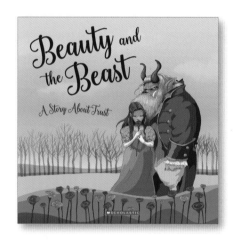

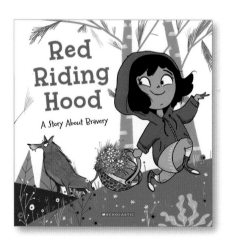